Grandma's Silent Auction
September
BY: Michael James

Copyright © 2020 by Michael James

All rights reserved.

No part of this book may be reproduced in any form or by any electronic or mechanical means, including information storage and retrieval systems, without written permission from the author, except for the use of brief quotations in a book review.

CHAPTER ONE
CIARA

I have spent the last two days in my room at Grams. Jeremy got me out of my store through the back entrance and into Grams car safely. We came right to the mansion, then I went right to my room and I haven't left it since. Grams has tried to get me to come out, but I don't feel like being in the same room with her. I'm pissed! She took my last night with Kirby away from me. I found that to be ridiculous. She's the one that hired this big, bad bodyguard to protect me, yet she didn't let him do his job when I wanted him to.

I haven't eaten since Kirby and I stopped off at that diner on our way home. Grams has sent Katie to bring me food, but I wasn't falling for that trick. I wasn't about to unlock my bedroom door and let her wiggle her way in to make up with me. The problem with that great plan, I'm starving and Katie hasn't tried to tempt me with her delicious muffins this morning. I have no other choice than to leave my room for food.

I open my door and peek my head out. Nobody is guarding my door. Not a single person in sight. Grams mansion is so big, there could be fifty people here and you wouldn't even know it. I wouldn't be surprised if someone was lurking around the corner in another hallway. It is probably childish of me to hide in my room. I know I am throwing a tantrum. It just really upsets me that everyone seems to think they know what is best for me without my input. That includes Kirby. He didn't much care for my opinion. It reminded me of getting put in a car and sent on my way just like Gaetano did to me. I'm not a child anymore. I wish people would stop treating me as if I am one. It makes me wonder when this is all said and done, will I get to actually be with the person I choose or will that be chosen for me? Am I going to be treated as an adult then? I have enough on my plate as it is. I don't need any more stress.

I make it to the kitchen without anyone noticing me. The mansion is completely quiet. I have to wonder, where the hell is everyone? I was at least expecting Jeremy to be lurking somewhere. It doesn't

CHAPTER 1

really matter. I can get some food and eat in peace, I guess.

I start rummaging through the cupboards for something to eat. I spot a can of tomato soup. Emm, soup with a grill cheese sandwich sounds appetizing. Perfect food for the soul.

※

It wasn't until I was down to the last bite of my grilled cheese sandwich that I got a glimpse of someone other than myself in the house. Katie came into the kitchen just when I was shoving the last bite in my mouth. She just looked at me and smiled, then went about her duties. I felt a tad guilty that she is cleaning up my mess.

"I can clean my mess, Katie. I'm sure you have other things you could be doing."

"It's fine, Ms. Verbank."

"Do you know where Grams is?"

"She stepped out."

"Do you know where she went?"

"I think she had a doctor's appointment."

Grams has had quite a few doctor appointments lately. I hope I am not being blind to something that could be something serious. She better not be keeping secrets from me about her health.

"Katie, is my Grandma sick?"

"I don't really know. Millie is a private person when it comes to stuff like that. She only tells me things that aren't that important."

"You haven't heard her slip up at all?"

"I wish I had the answers you seek, but I have nothing to give you."

"Do you know where Jeremy is?"

"Oh yes, he's in the study."

"Thanks," I say walking out of the kitchen.

I don't really care to talk to Jeremy, but I need to see if he might know where Grams went off to. I'm worried about her. If she's keeping a huge secret from me, I'm not going to be happy at all. That's just wrong on many levels. When it comes right down to it, I'm all she has. If she's sick, I have the right to know.

Before I can even enter the study, I can hear Jeremy's voice. Either he's talking to himself or he's on the phone with someone. He doesn't seem like the type of person to talk to himself, so I'll go with the latter.

As I enter the room, he sees me right away. He tells the person he has to go and that he'll see whoever at one. I peek my eyes over to the grandfather clock, it's already past one in the afternoon. Is he sneaking out in the early hours of the morning?

I casually walk around the study. *"Going somewhere?"*

"Glad to see you emerged from your room finally."

I just love how he avoided my question. *"Didn't really think you'd give a shit."* He snickers. *"It's no secret you don't like me."*

Jeremy takes his glasses off. Damn, he looks sexy in glasses. I didn't realize he wore them. Not once in the past month did I see him wear glasses. The dark frames look great with his light blond hair color. They do hide his striking blue eyes a little, though.

"Is that what you think?"

I shake my head to clear my thoughts when he speaks. I don't need to be checking out my bodyguard. I have enough men to think about.

"It is what I think," I say as I come around the desk to see what is on his laptop. Just like last time, he closed the lid before I could get a glimpse of what he's doing. I park my ass on the corner of the desk. *"That is exactly what I think,"* I repeat.

"You have the wrong opinion on what I think about you."

"Oh really? What is your opinion of me, Jeremy?"

Jeremy stands and places his hands on the desk, caging my body between his arms. *"I think you are a spoiled brat. Is that what you want to hear?"*

"Oh keep going, this is getting interesting."

"You think you have me all figured out, don't you Ms. Verbank?" He leans in closer to my face. I get chills when his mouth goes near my ear. *"You don't have a clue what I think about you. You know nothing about what goes on inside my head."*

I look him in the eyes when his face comes back into view. *"So you do or you don't think I'm a spoiled brat? Don't be shy, just tell me. I can handle the truth."*

"I don't have time for this today."

"Why is that? Do you need to prepare for your early morning getaway?"

"Eavesdropping doesn't suit you. I thought you were better than that. Just in case your curious mind really needs to know, yes, I need to prepare for later."

I get chills again when his arms drop off the desk and he stands straight up, the smell of his cologne going with him. Jeremy is such a big man. I bet he could bench press me without breaking a

CHAPTER 1

sweat. I would feel sorry for anyone who'd mess with him.

"Who were you talking to when I came in?"

"A friend of mine."

"Does this friend have a name? Is it a girlfriend?"

"Don't you have packing to do?"

"Avoiding the question. I'm just going to assume it's a girlfriend."

He throws his head back as he laughs. When he stops laughing he casually walks away. *"If you'll excuse me, I have important shit to do. We'll talk about this later."*

I hop off the desk. *"Jeremy, wait. Do you know where my Grandma went?"*

"To an appointment."

"Do you know where?"

"I do not."

This time when he heads to the door, I don't stop him. I wait until he's long gone before I start snooping in Grams desk. There's got to be a clue around here somewhere about what's going on with her. I eye Jeremy's laptop on the desk. I look toward the door and back to it. I open the lid and run my finger along the touchpad. Of course, it needs a pin!

"What are you doing?"

No use lying. *"Spying on you!"*

"8675309"

"Huh?"

"The pin."

"Oh," I say each number as I hit each key. I narrow my eyes at him when I realize what numbers he gave me. He just stands there smiling like a jackass.

"Can I have my laptop now?"

I close the cover and hand it to him. *"I'm sorry. I haven't ever done something like that. I don't know what I was thinking."*

I jump up from the desk and run out of the study. Seriously, what is wrong with me? I hear him say my name, but I keep running toward my room. I can't believe I just did that. I would be pissed if someone tried to invade my privacy like that. I don't even want to think about if it were Grams who caught me snooping through her things. She taught me not to snoop where my nose didn't belong. She would be disappointed in me without question. Honestly, I feel really bad about what I just did.

I slam my door shut and lock it. I am so angry at myself that I want to be left alone. I throw myself on top of the bed. Nobody needs to see me bawling my eyes out anyway. Even though I deserve the humiliation I would receive if someone saw me this way.

I sit up and wipe my eyes. It just hit me what Jeremy said about packing. Shit! I have to leave in the morning to go off and meet another guy. I get off my bed and start looking for the three-ring binder. I have no idea who the hell I'm meeting. When I find it on top of my dresser, I open it and flip through the pages to September. I read his name, Wyatt Bradshaw. I'm flying off to Pennsylvania.

CHAPTER TWO
CIARA

I was in my room for the last couple of hours reflecting on my actions the past couple of days. I've been wandering around the mansion looking for Jeremy, but I can't seem to find him anywhere. I am still upset with myself for attempting to look at Jeremy's laptop. I feel I owe him another apology. I also feel that maybe it's time for Grams and I to have a heart to heart conversation. I need to know if I should be concerned about her health. She isn't a spring chicken even if she wants to pretend she is. Grams has always been young at heart and super active, but health issues tend to sneak up on people no matter one's age. Since I can't seem to find Jeremy anywhere I might as well go and talk with Grams. I saw her not too long ago going into her bedroom.

I knock on her door and tell her it's me. When she doesn't answer, I peek my head inside. I don't see her, but I walk in anyway. She sometimes likes to go out on her balcony. Grams is big on watching the sunset.

"Hi, Grams."

"Hello, sweetheart."

"Can I join you?"

"Of course you can."

I step out onto the balcony, then sit next to her. *"Beautiful night out."*

"It is. I take it you are done being mad at me."

"I was looking for you this afternoon and Katie told me you went to the doctor."

"I did. Just a normal checkup."

"You would tell me if something serious was going on, right?"

Her eyes lower. *"If you are asking if I'm sick, I am fine."*

"Is that the truth? My gut is telling me you are not fine."

"Ciara, if there were something serious going on with my health, I'd tell you."

She lifts her eyes and stares out at the setting sun. I don't have a choice but to believe her. Clearly if my gut intuition is right, she isn't going to tell me. For now, I have to pretend she's fine and pray she isn't lying to me.

"Do you know where Jeremy is?" I laugh a little. *"Did you fire him?"*

"No, I didn't fire him. He was just sitting where you are not long before you came out here."

I guess that explains why I didn't find him. Grams bedroom is the last place I'd look for him. I peek at her from the corner of my eye. I can't shake the unsettling feeling she's keeping something from me.

"I'm going to find something to eat."

"It would have been nice if you would have come to dinner the last few nights. Maybe next time you are home you won't be locking yourself in your room."

"I was angry at many things. I just needed time alone to regroup."

"I know this adventure I put you on has been trying at times. I wouldn't have taken your last night away from Kirby if I didn't feel your safety was at risk. I hope you find true love at the end of this or I made the biggest mistake of my life. I have faith it will work itself out, though."

I get to my feet. *"I have found love, Grams. More than once. I was angry because I didn't let Kirby in. I waited too long because I was scared to fall for another one of your guys and have them fall for me. I needed that last night with him."*

"I hope you haven't been avoiding his attempts to

CHAPTER 2

contact you then. Don't ignore a man for doing what was right."

"Good night, Grams." I bend to kiss her cheek.

"I had Katie put a plate of dinner in the refrigerator for you."

I nod my head. Nobody knows me the way she does. I have in fact ignored Kirby's attempts to talk to me because I've been upset with him for leaving the way he did.

Instead of going to find Jeremy like I was planning on, I came to the kitchen after I went to my room to get my phone. These past few days, I've been a fool. I need to return his call. I need to hear him out and find out why he left the way he did.

I find the plate Katie had made for me and pop it in the microwave. Leaning against the counter, I scroll through my recent call list to find Kirby's number. I am quite surprised to see I missed a call from Lincoln. I press the missed call notification and call him. I am curious to find out why he called me. I cross my fingers that nothing bad has happened. I don't think I could handle any more bad news.

"Hello, Ciara."

"Hello. I see I missed a call from you."

"I know it's against the rules Millie set to keep in

contact, but I am home for a few days and started thinking about you."

"Is that a good thing or a bad thing?"

"Always a good thing. I am getting on a flight to the city in a little bit. I should be there in a couple of hours. I was wondering if you are home. I'd love to see you. Maybe tomorrow?"

"I am home, but I'm leaving in the morning to go to Pennsylvania."

"I feel like I'm a day late and a dollar short."

"What time are you getting in?"

"It won't be until around midnight if everything goes according to plan."

"Call me when you land. Maybe I can sneak you into the mansion."

"I'll do that. I hope to see you later. I miss being with you."

"My fingers are crossed."

We say goodbye and I get my dinner from the microwave and carry it to the table with me. Hearing Lincoln wanting to see me, makes me want to set things straight with Kirby even more. After taking a few bites of my dinner, I hit the call button next to his name. My nerves spike as I wait for him to answer.

"I was beginning to think you'd never return my calls."

CHAPTER 2

I smile at the sound of his voice. *"I'm sorry it took me so long to call you back."*

"Are you alright?"

"Can I be honest with you?"

"I wouldn't want you to be dishonest with me."

"I am not alright with the way things were left between us. I really wanted our last night together to mean something to you."

"Ciara, our entire time together meant the world to me. Being with you has shown me the type of person you are. It showed me relationships are possible with my line of work."

"You don't understand."

"What don't I understand?"

"I held back on letting you in. I was scared to share my past with you. I was scared to open myself up and think about what kind of future we could have together."

"You gave me enough about you to know you are a beautiful person inside and out. You care about the little things and see life in ways many don't. Do I know every little detail about what makes you the person you are? The answer is no. I can tell men have belittled you into believing you are not worthy of genuine love."

"Don't you need more from me to decide if I'm the

right person for you? You shared so much of yourself with me."

"We can have a lifetime together learning more and more about each other. You made me want to be the man that shows you how a man should love a woman. If I am the man you want, I want to be with you."

"What if you find out you don't like what I haven't shared with you?"

"I find myself believing that your past isn't going to change my feelings. I saw who you are as a person, Ciara, and I'm in love with you. I'm sorry I left the way I did. I wish the outcome was different. I'm not very good at goodbyes."

"You know how you took me to the top of the hill and told me it was your special place?"

"Yes."

"I don't have anything like that in my life. I don't know who my father is. I have a mother who hates me. What if I end up being a bad wife or mother because of what I went through. We are different in that aspect of how we grew up."

"I read people for a living. You are going to be a terrific wife and mother someday. You learned from your heartache. You'll be the exact opposite of your mother. Millie did right by you."

CHAPTER 2

"You sound pretty confident about that."

"Because I am." There is a little silence between us. *"I hate to do this, but I have to go. I'm about to board a plane."*

"Where are you going?"

"I have a poker game in Vegas tomorrow."

"Same place?"

"Nah, it's a private game at one of my fellow competitor's homes."

"Good luck. I'm glad we talked."

"Have a good night, Ciara. I'm looking forward to the next time we can be together."

How he gets me, I don't understand. Maybe he can read me better than I can read myself. Kirby is an incredible person through and through. I have nothing negative to say about him. I almost think he might be too good of a person to be with a girl like me. Maybe all these men Grams handpicked for me deserve a woman who has their shit together completely.

※

I feel a hand on my shoulder, shaking me. At first I thought I was just dreaming, then I heard Jeremy's voice tell me to wake up. After it sinks in he's in my room, my eyes pop open. Fear courses through me as I think something is wrong with Grams. I sat up in a hurry and asked what was wrong.

"We have to go."

I pull the covers back as I swing my legs over the edge and reach for the bedside lamp. *"Why? What is going on?"*

"I'm getting you out of New York."

"That isn't telling me much. You're scaring me."

"I have a way to get you out of here so that no one can follow you."

"Where are we going?"

"Pennsylvania."

"Wyatt's?"

"Yes." He looks at what I'm wearing. *"I'll be waiting in the hall while you get dressed. You have five minutes."*

Five minutes! Christ, he wakes me in the middle of the night and gives me only five minutes to leave! This man drives me absolutely insane.

I quickly throw on some clothes. I don't see what's so urgent, me leaving in the middle of the night is a little confusing. It's not like the media won't find out my whereabouts and tell the whole world where I am. All of Grams' men are high profile guys and the media loves to invade people's privacy.

Jeremy takes the small bag I packed. His

CHAPTER 2 19

eyebrows raised like he's surprised I packed so little. I follow him through the halls and down the main staircase. When we reached the back door, my eyebrows were the ones being raised. My heart rate picks up.

"I'm not getting on that helicopter."

"Yes, you are, Ciara."

"What are you going to do, throw me over your shoulder if I refuse?"

"If I must." I roll my eyes. He can kiss my ass. *"I know you don't like flying. Your grandmother and I think this is the best way to keep your stalker guessing. It will help us in the long run."*

"I don't see how."

"I promise you will soon enough."

"Fine, if I die or throw up, it's your fault." He laughs. What a jerk! He opens the door for me to get in. *"Umm, who is flying this thing?"*

"I am!"

Just fucking great! I'm putting my life in the hands of a guy who doesn't like me much! I cross my fingers he likes himself well enough to not kill us. I fasten my seatbelt and he hands me a set of headphones. I look at him as he starts flipping switches.

"Relax," he says, *"I've flown many times and know what I'm doing."*

"The way you checked your seatbelt three times

on the flight to Kirby's, I didn't think you liked flying as much as I don't."

"I wasn't checking it. I was making it looser."

"Oh!"

"Close your eyes if you wish, but flying in a helicopter is pretty cool, especially at night."

Close my eyes! No fucking way! I need to see if we are about to crash. What if he doesn't see a tall building or something? I need to know when to scream.

˜

Jeremy was great at keeping me calm. It was kind of cool to see the city below us all lit up. I might prefer to fly this way instead of in a plane. When we landed, he announced we were here. I couldn't believe how fast we got to Pennsylvania.

When we reached the front door of Wyatt's home, I was once again surprised. Jeremy didn't knock. In fact he had a key to get inside. He showed me to the bedroom I'll be staying in and told me he'll see me in the morning. Just like that he left me alone in a strange place. Where the hell is Wyatt? How did Jeremy get a key? How does he expect me to sleep after a night like this?

CHAPTER THREE
CIARA

It took me hours to feel comfortable enough to try and get more sleep. It's hard enough to sleep in someone's home when you barely know a person, let alone not knowing the person at all. But, I did manage to finally get a couple more hours in. Nothing in specific woke me up, I just woke on my own. I got out of bed and took a shower. I figured there is no rush for me to leave this room. Honestly, I don't like the way I'm meeting Wyatt. I would have much rather met at the airport, an office or another way. Any way except this. I mean really, what am I supposed to do, get all dolled up and walk out of this room and yell, here I am!? Well that isn't going to happen. I'm not going out of my way to introduce myself to a man who couldn't be around when I arrived at his home. Hell, I landed on the guy's lawn, you'd think that he'd be waiting for my arrival. You don't just toss a woman in a man's house and be done with it.

I jump when I hear a knock on the door. I could pretend to still be asleep. Make him wait to meet me until I'm goddamn ready.

"Ciara, are you awake?"

"Jeremy?"

"I made breakfast if you are hungry."

First he has a key and now he made breakfast. I whip the door open. *"Are you friends with Wyatt or something?"*

"Or something." He looks away then back to me. *"Are you hungry? I made waffles."*

"Toaster waffles?"

"No, homemade ones. I have strawberries and blueberries or you can have it with syrup."

I can smell the aroma of bacon floating down the hallway. *"I smell bacon."* I step out of the room. *"You should have mentioned bacon first,"* I say to him from over my shoulder.

I get to the end of the hallway and the home opens up to a huge open floor plan. The kitchen is to my right, living room to my left. There is another hallway across the way. I go toward the kitchen as I take in how bright the sun shines in. The walls are made of all windows. The floors are gray hardwood and the

CHAPTER 3

furniture is white with black accents. It feels homey enough, even though it feels like I'm stepping into a home that belongs in a showcase.

I sit at the breakfast bar where Jeremy has our breakfast spread out very nicely. I peek at him from the corner of my eye. He did all this for me?

"I boiled water in case you wanted tea instead of coffee. I know you prefer tea."

"That I do. What kinds are there?"

He pushes a basket toward me. I pick through it and find it's all the flavors I love. I choose the one I want and open the wrapping, dunking it into the hot water.

"Did you get more sleep?"

"A little. How about you?"

"I passed right out. I was exhausted."

"How did you get a key?"

"Eat, Ciara, the food is getting cold."

There's my bodyguard being all short with me again. I think I like the guy who made me breakfast much more. Jeremy is a tough person to figure out. I should just give up trying. He's not going to be my bodyguard forever, so there is no use trying to be friends anyway.

I fill my plate with a waffle, then add butter and syrup. I take my first bite and it's delicious. I get a couple slices of bacon. Jeremy slides the syrup back over to me after he uses it. I pour a little on each strip. I have to assume he knows how I like my bacon.

"This is really good."

"Thank you. The neighbor lady taught me how to make the waffles when I was a kid."

"Did she teach you anything else?"

"I got all my cooking skills from her."

"What about your mother? Did she teach you anything?"

"Ya, how to put a TV dinner in the oven."

"Oh."

"Before you ask, I didn't have a father to teach me squat."

"I know what that is like."

"I know."

I sense Jeremy is getting uncomfortable with our conversation. For once I don't blame him. When it comes to sharing about my own parents, it makes me nauseous. Who wants to tell anyone your mom never said who your father is and then abandoned you a few years later. I have a feeling Jeremy would totally get how I feel. It sounds like his mom didn't leave him, but wasn't much of a mother. In my book it might as well be the same thing.

"I always thought I'd be a horrible mother.

CHAPTER 3

Recently I was told I'd be the opposite of what my parents were."

"You were raised by someone who loves you. You will take more away from that than what your mother did to you."

"How about you? Do you think you'll be a good father?"

"I like to think I'll be. I learned what type of parent I don't want to be just like you did."

That is the most he's ever opened up to me. Hell, it is probably the most he's ever talked to me at one time. If he could be this nice person all the time, I think we could be friends.

We finish our breakfast in silence. When I was finished, I started to clean up. Jeremy told me to leave it. He got up from the breakfast bar himself and took the dirty plate from my hand, setting it on the counter. He then proceeded to clear off the breakfast bar, leaving the dishes by the sink. I start to wander around Wyatt's home, wondering when he'll make an appearance. I spot a framed picture on the fireplace mantle. I walk right over to it. When I get close enough to see it, my jaw drops. It's a photo of Jeremy and a woman. I spin around and he's standing right behind me. I'm so stunned, I don't know what to say. His eyes go to the floor as he runs a hand through his hair.

"What's going on here? Do you know the man who lives here?"

"I know him very well."

"And?"

"Come outside with me. It's a beautiful morning."

"Jeremy, stop with being short with me. Whenever I ask you a question you mostly avoid answering them. I'm at my wits end with you."

"Just come outside with me."

"I don't want to go outside."

"I'm going out there. If you want answers that's where I'll be."

I watch him walk to the door and go outside. Ugh! He makes my head spin. I glance at the picture one last time before putting it back where I found it. Jeremy looks very happy in the photo. If I want to know what the hell is going on, I have to go outside.

Jeremy is sitting in a rocking chair waiting for me to join him. I don't, though. I look around at the outdoor view and take in the morning sun. He's right, it is a beautiful day out. I eventually turn and lean my ass against the porch railing, crossing my arms across my upper body. I hope he sees how irritated I am. I stare at him. I'm not talking until he gives me some answers.

"You asked me earlier how I got a key to this house. The key is mine."

"Fine, I have a key to Porter's apartment. Nothing unusual about that. What I don't get is why you avoided answering the question like it's a big secret."

"I told you yesterday you know nothing about me. If I have been stand-offish it isn't because I wanted to be. It hasn't been easy being your bodyguard."

"It hasn't been easy for me either, but I've been trying to be friends at least. We are kinda stuck with each other for the time being."

"Ciara, it was difficult for me because I'm not Jeremy. I am Wyatt Bradshaw. It was not fun watching the woman you would soon be dating be with another man."

I don't even know what to say. This has to be a joke! I don't know if I want to shake him until he tells me he's kidding, or slap him across the face. I'm sure he deserves the latter for lying to me for an entire month. How in the world do they think this is okay? Whose bright idea was this, his or Grams? All I know, whoever came up with this has lost their damn mind. How in the world am I supposed to build a relationship with Wyatt after he saw me with Kirby. This isn't fair to either one of us. I don't see how a relationship can form between us.

"Would you say something?"

I laugh out of nervousness. *"So, let me get this straight. You were Jeremy my bodyguard, and now you are Wyatt my boyfriend for the month. Will you be Jeremy again next month?"*

"I didn't want to be Jeremy. Millie asked for my help finding you a bodyguard. Everyone I trust was already on jobs. I wasn't about to let Millie hire someone neither one of us knew. If it were anyone else, I wouldn't have cared."

"Is that supposed to make me feel better?"

"You know damn well that if you knew I was the guy who you'd date this month it would have strained your relationship with Kirby. It would have been more awkward for you than it was for me."

I push off the porch railing. I need time for this to sink in. As I go to pass Wyatt, he grabs my hand and stands up from the rocker.

"Just don't, Wyatt. I don't even get why you brought me here. You don't even like me half the time."

"You still think that? What I don't like is watching the girl I'm going to be in a relationship with, kissing

another man. I don't fucking share. You have no idea what I think, so quit assuming what I think about you."

His blue eyes are staring into my brown ones with so much power. I swallow hard, even though my mouth has gone dry. *"You have a funny way of showing you like someone then, because I could swear you ...."*

My words are hushed by the impact of his lips slamming into mine. My heart is thumping in my chest as his mouth takes over mine. I grip onto the upper sleeves of his shirt as I let myself kiss him back. I feel my anger fading the longer he kisses me. I am breathless by the time his mouth leaves mine.

"I don't kiss women like that if I don't like them." He steps backward three steps before turning around and walking off the porch.

"Where are you going?"

"To cool off."

"Are you mad at me again?"

"Nope! If I don't walk away right now, I'd probably carry your ass into the house and strip you from your clothing."

"Oh," I say softly, knowing he didn't hear me.

CHAPTER FOUR
WYATT

Ciara is goddamn crazy to think I don't like her! If that kiss didn't prove to her just how much I'm attracted to her, nothing will. That woman has no idea how badly I've wanted to kiss her during the last month. Instead I had to sit by and watch her getting all chummy with Kirby. I've seen shit that has burned my ass, but nothing compares to watching the woman you are about to date be with another man. It was like being back in high school where your buddy got the girl you wanted and you knew you could never date her after that. It wasn't easy by any means watching Ciara be with Kirby. I had to keep telling myself not to leave last month. I wanted to a few times, but I couldn't just abandon Ciara. She needs my protection from this psychopath who's after her. Hell, I wouldn't abandon any woman in this situation, that's not who I am. I have every intent to find out who this person is before this month is over with. I don't think I could watch her be with another man after being with me this month.

I cannot shake that kiss from my mind. Damn, it was better than I ever could have imagined. I am not a guy who falls for a woman very easily. It takes me a long time to trust anyone. Male or female, but especially female. I've had my ass burnt too many times by the female gender, starting at a very young age. My mother was the first one who showed me you can't trust easily. Let's just say I've dated a few women who I never should've trusted. Don't get me wrong, I know not all people are bad. There are trustworthy people in this big old world, you just have to search a little harder to find them. Ciara is one of the good ones. I saw firsthand the kind of person she is. It's probably why I'm so attracted to her. Well that and she is gorgeous. Ciara doesn't have a clue how many men wish they had a chance with her. She turns heads and doesn't even realize it. If she did, she never would have dated Hunter. That little fucker is treading on thin ice with me. If he's not careful, I'll be the one to crack the ice. He'll fall through it before he can even blink. Trust me when I say, if he's behind what's been happening to Ciara, I'll find out. I'm good at what I do. Hunting criminals is what I do very well. I have all the resources that I need at my fingertips.

❧

I went for a long walk. I needed to cool off and I'm sure Ciara needed time to let who I am sink in. I'm sure her mind is going a mile a minute about everything that has transpired. I've had an entire month to know this was going to happen. She's only had the last hour while I've been walking. Now that she knows I'm Wyatt, I'm hopeful we can begin our relationship. I've been looking forward to her learning who I am. I know it isn't going to be a breeze. I have some making up to do. There may be a few things I have up my sleeve to help win her over. As I said, I have resources at my fingertips. If luck is on my side, I just might be the one who saves her from herself with all the doubt that lies in her thoughts.

When I step into my house, Ciara isn't in the main part of it. My cleaning lady is in the kitchen, though, washing the dishes from breakfast. I haven't seen her in a while.

"Hello, Angela."
"Hello, Mr. Bradshaw."

CHAPTER 4

"How are you and the family?"

"Very well, thank you."

"Is Garret off to college to play ball?"

"He is. He left last week. I'm to tell you he says thank you for the care package. It was very kind of you."

"It was nothing. I can remember when I went off to college without a dime in my pocket. I know you saved, but I'm hoping my help gives him more time to study instead of working at some job."

"I'm sure it will. He's determined to show you he'll get good grades."

"I have no doubt he'll do well."

"It didn't go unnoticed, the extra money in my paycheck. You are too kind to us. Thank you."

"I know you are a single mother. It's not always easy on you. I'm happy to help you out."

"I bought the boys school clothes, so it was very helpful."

"Are you about done here?"

"I am. I'm going to the office next."

"Good. If you see Becks, give him hell for me. Tell him to stop leaving his coffee cups everywhere." She smiles. *"Have you seen a pretty lady floating around here?"*

"I have. She's hiding in the guest bedroom. She's very sweet."

"That she is."

I walk away and head toward my bedroom. I hear Ciara call out my name from behind. I turn around and she is charging after me. It's hard to take my eyes off her. She clearly didn't change from the t-shirt she slept in.

"Wyatt, you don't get to kiss me like that and walk away."

I glance at Angela. Ciara crosses the room at a steady pace. I look back at my cleaning lady, she dries her hands then grabs her keys off the counter to make her exit. By the time Angela leaves, Ciara is standing in front of me, with her hands on her hips. She's cute when being all flustered.

"Don't just stand there and stare at me."

What does she expect me to do? Good grief does this woman not know how turned on I am right now? The way her breasts freely moved as she walked? *"What else should I be doing?"*

"Oh gee, I don't know! How about you explain to me why you took it upon yourself to kiss me then walk away."

"I already told you why I walked away."

She takes the few steps that are left between us

and puts her hands to my shoulders, then gives me a shove. It is laughable that she thought she could move me. I don't laugh though, I keep that to myself.

She lets out a huff. *"Don't kiss me again!"*

Ciara tried to push me again. This time I grabbed both her wrists as they dropped from my shoulder. Her eyes go wide, then they narrow at me. I look at her mouth. Her lips tremor, tempting me to kiss her once again.

"I won't unless you want me to."

"Not in this lifetime would I want you to put your mouth on…"

The impact of my lips on hers, hushes the words coming out of her delicious mouth. When my mouth takes over hers, she isn't fighting me. Her hands come to my neck, then her fingers comb into my hair. Her body presses tightly against mine. This doesn't seem like a woman who doesn't want to be kissed. Then suddenly her mouth is gone. She looks me in the eyes while her hands drop. This time when our bodies part, it is her that walks away.

"Where are you going?" I ask with a smile on my face.

"Away from you," she snaps back.

"For a woman who didn't want me to kiss her again in this lifetime, it sure didn't feel that way."

She spins back around on her heels and comes charging back after me. *"I could..."*

I grab her by the waist when she is close to me and bring her body to mine. *"You could what?"*

I let her go when she doesn't answer me. If I were a betting man, I'd say she wanted to slap me.

"You are fucking insane, you know that? I want to leave."

"The door is right over there."

I close the inch that is between us and she steps back. I keep moving with her until her back hits the wall. I put my arms up, caging her between them. She gasps.

"What are you doing?"

"What do you want me to do, Ciara?"

Ciara grabs the back of my neck, her body leaping into mine as her mouth slams onto mine. I move and press her back against the wall again. Our kiss is heated. I can't tell who is in control at this point. Good fucking God, I want this woman underneath me, stripped naked and calling out my name as I bring her to orgasm.

Both of us need air. Her more than me. I put my hands on her upper arms and pin them to the wall. I bend my upper body, putting my mouth over her breast, then suck on her erect nipple. She moans when

CHAPTER 4

I bite down before moving over to the other breast. I glance at the wet spots on her shirt before I stand up straight and kiss her neck while I drop her arms from my grip. I'm giving her one last shot to walk away. To my surprise, she reached up and slapped me across the face. Did I deserve that? Maybe. I should walk away, but my feet stay planted where they are. We just stare at each other for a few moments. I think she's just as surprised about slapping me as I was. It would be very wise of me to put some distance between us. I may want Ciara, however, I don't want her to regret having sex with me. I reluctantly begin to walk the rest of the way to my room.

Fuck, I need a cold shower. I get inside my room and strip from my shirt. I am undoing the button on my jeans when her voice enters my room.

"I'm sorry. I shouldn't have ..."

Her words trail off when I turn to face her standing in the doorway. *"Shouldn't have what?"*

I notice the wet rings around her nipples on her shirt. I tell myself to stop torturing myself and my eyes travel back to hers. She reaches for the hem, then takes her shirt off. This time it's me who goes charging after her. I lift her off her feet and carry her across the room, tossing her to my bed. Both of us frantically remove our pants. I get on the bed between her legs and kiss her. She takes a hold of my manhood and puts it to her pussy. In one hard thrust, I'm inside her. I suck in a breath, as she did at my intrusion. Fucking hell, she's tight around my cock. Like a mad man, I fuck her hard. My mind doesn't know what gentle is at the moment. Her lower lips gripping my shaft is telling me, Ciara doesn't seem to mind the roughness. In fact, I think she likes it rough. Angry sex has its way to turn people on and we are no different than other people.

Ciara bites my neck as her pussy quivers. Her orgasm doesn't take long to come. Honestly, neither does mine. Being inside her is absolutely amazing. Better than any other woman I've been with. I could do this all day and night and not be completely over wanting to fuck her. I have a feeling the more sex we have, the more I'll want. This woman has me and that's a scary thought to have.

CHAPTER FIVE
CIARA

Holy hell that was intense! Wyatt rolls off of me and the loss of his body heat gives me chills. I think that was anger and attraction all rolled up into one hell of a sexual experience. I would be lying if I said I didn't enjoy every goddamn second of it. I just might have to stay mad at him the entire month if the sex is going to be like that. That was truly out of this world amazing.

I turn my head to look in his direction. I'm still upset that he lied to me about who he was. Having him naked next to me helps with that anger, though. It's not like it was entirely his fault. I mean, I'm sure Grams gave him the bright idea to tell me his name was Jeremy.

"*I'm hungry,*" he announces. "*Are you?*"

"*I'm sure I could eat.*"

"*Good.*"

Wyatt gets off the bed and grabs his jeans. After he slips them on, he only does up a few buttons. He faces the bed and my eyes go to the defined V-shape his muscles form. Button fly jeans only done halfway up with defined muscles trying to hide, now that is sexy as hell.

"My eyes are up here, Ciara."

"I could have said that to you earlier when you couldn't stop looking at my chest."

"Fair enough."

I squeal when he grabs my ankles and drags my body down to the foot of the bed. *"Do you cook?"*

"Not much."

"Get dressed. I'll teach you one of my favorite meals to make." He bends over my body and kisses me. *"You keep looking at me like that, food might have to wait."* He stands straight up, once again leaving me with chills.

"That would be such a shame, huh?"

"Not really."

I sit up on the bed and grab the waistband of his jeans, tugging him toward me. I put my lips to his flat, hard stomach. His hand comes to my chin, lifting my face to look at him. I undo the few buttons he did up and then push his jeans past his hips. His manhood is starting to get hard all over again. I take his cock in my hand and stroke him until he's fully erect. I slide off the end of the bed and get on my knees. I lick my lips before I take him in my mouth. I take him in as far as I can before sliding his cock along my tongue on the way back out. Sucking him back and using my tongue, he groans. His hand grips onto my hair. I place my hands on his hips as he starts to take over my mouth only allowing him in so far. My pussy quivers at the thought of him being back inside me. I'm not done yet, though. I want his cum on my tongue first. I close my lips tighter around his girth, then drop my hands from his hips, allowing him more control. He thrusts and his cock goes to my throat. I am rewarded with his orgasm a few strokes later. I get to my feet, and he quickly spins me around and bends me over the foot of the bed. Entering me from behind, I gasp. His arms wrap around my waist, picking me up, my knees press into the mattress when he sets me down. With my face against the blankets, he grabs my arms and pins my hands to my lower back. My entire body jolts forward as he re-enters with a hard thrust.

Wyatt is relentless as he fucks me and I am loving every second of what he is doing to my body. I like what he is doing so much so that I announce I'm cumming. That doesn't slow his pace, though. In fact, he goes faster. I am so far gone by the time his release comes, that I fall flat to the bed when he lets go of my hands.

Wyatt falls to the bed next to me. Through his labored breaths, he says, *"Holy fuck, Ciara, you may be the death of me."*

Death of him? He might kill me with orgasm overload. I'm too out of breath to say anything, so I just lie here and get my breathing under control.

❧

Wyatt gets all the ingredients out to make dinner. I eye the different spices and food that needs to be cut, diced or whatever. Practically the entire counter is used. I know how to cook, but I mostly used jarred or canned goods with meat added in. I make nothing entirely from scratch. I see a fresh loaf of Italian bread and would have to assume Angela whom I met earlier did some shopping for Wyatt before our arrival. I didn't see her bring any bags in when she got here today, though.

"What are we making again?"

"Fiesta Lime Chicken."

"Right! So where do we start?"

"First we must make the marinade for the chicken."

"Where's the recipe?"

"Right here," he says, pointing to his head.

We make the marinade, homemade salsa to use in a cream sauce, then put everything in the refrigerator to set for a couple of hours. Once everything we used is put back in its place, I ask what everything else is for. Wyatt said you can't make a dinner from scratch without having a homemade dessert to go along with it. So we proceeded to make a New York style cheesecake. When it's in the oven, Wyatt opens a bottle of wine and pours two glasses.

"Come with me outside?"

"Why, Wyatt Bradshaw, did you actually ask me to do something instead of telling me?"

"I might have," he answers smiling.

Wyatt takes my hand and pulls me to him. He runs a finger along the inside of the bowl, filling it with cheesecake filling. He puts his finger to my mouth and I lick the filling off. He kisses me and groans. I think I just fell in love with cheesecake even more. I've always been a fan, but this is way better than I've ever had.

We go outside and I follow him around the corner of the porch. We take a staircase and at the top is an open deck on the roof. You can see mountains off in the distance in every direction. It's really a fantastic view. Wyatt has a seat at one of the many chairs, kicking his feet up. I walk around the entire deck, taking in the fresh air. I bet Grams would love it here. To sit in the open and watch the sun set off in the horizon.

I finally have a seat next to Wyatt. He picks up his glass of wine and holds it up in front of him.

"Welcome to my home, Ciara."

I hold mine up and tell him thank you. Since we had sex, twice, I feel my anger toward him melting away. I don't know where our relationship will go from here, but I cannot deny I am extremely attracted to him. The sexual chemistry between us is undeniable. Time will tell if there will be more to us than that.

"So tell me, Wyatt, am I really the first person you became a bodyguard to?"

"You are."

"So what is it you really do for a living?"

"I am a US deputy marshal and I own one of the largest companies in Pennsylvania."

"A marshal , as in you bring in criminals?"

"That would be correct."

"How many have you caught?"

"Too many to count. I'm semi-retired now. I only go after the hard core cases that others can't handle."

"Have you had to kill?"

"A handful of times, yes."

"Wow, I don't think I could ever do that."

He sets his glass down on a table between us. *"I believe anyone could when the choice is kill or be killed."*

"What is your business?"

"It's sort of hard to explain. Maybe we can go into my office tomorrow and I can show you."

"I'd like that."

I lean back and kick my feet up. Sipping on my wine, I think about him being a marshal. That has got to be a dangerous job. It makes sense now why Grams would want Wyatt to be my bodyguard.

CHAPTER SIX
WYATT

After dinner last night, Ciara and I watched the sunset, then we curled up in my bed and watched a movie. She fell asleep halfway through it. I couldn't sleep, so I slipped out of bed without waking her and got on the computer. I was so engrossed into what I was doing I didn't realize a few hours had passed until my buddy, Becks, called. He is known to call all hours of the day and night. We talked for quite a while about a case he's on. He tried hard to get me on the case, but I declined. I am not about to give up time with Ciara to go on a manhunt. I took a leave for a reason. I caved a little, I told him I'd do what I could from home in my spare time.

This morning when I woke, Ciara was still sleeping peacefully, so I got out of bed, made coffee for myself and made sure everything was set for Ciara's tea. I'm not going to lie, I wanted to wake her.

CHAPTER 6

I learned in the last month that she isn't much of a morning person. She can tend to be a little grumpy if she is woken up before she wants to be.

I brought my coffee up to the roof. I really enjoy my mornings out here. There's nothing like fresh air to start your day off on the right foot. I'd spend most of my day up here if I could. Usually by the time I watch the sun come up and drink my coffee, my phone starts ringing, alerting me it's time to work. With me going semi-retired from the Marshal service, I get to enjoy my morning a little longer before I get busy with running my business. Sometimes it feels it's all work and no play. I love what I do. At the end of the day I can honestly say I did good in the world.

I am at a good place in my life and I'm ready to take the next step. I'm ready to find love, get married, and have some kids. I'm ready to show the world you can overcome obstacles and better yourself. With dedication and hard work you can live a wonderful life with happiness.

It warms my heart when I see Ciara at the top of the staircase. It's hard to believe she thought I didn't like her. Even though she was with another man last month, I got a chance to get to know her a little. I tried to mind my own business, but she made it difficult to ignore her. I felt myself wanting to know her on a deeper level. I haven't felt that way for a woman in a long time. My plan is to show her just how much I already care about her. I didn't ever believe there was this thing called love at first sight, holy hell, she proved me wrong. Her coming into Millie's kitchen in only a t-shirt and undies, I thought to myself, she's the one for me. I don't fully understand that thought, and it had nothing to do with what she was wearing. A feeling swooped in inside of me that I just knew I would fall for her and want to be the man she comes home to everyday.

"Good morning."

"Good morning, beautiful."

"Thank you for getting the stuff ready for my tea."

"You're welcome. Did you sleep well?"

"I slept like a rock. How long have you been up?"

"A little over an hour."

"While I was waiting for the water to get hot for my tea, I remembered seeing a photo of you and a woman on the mantel. If you don't mind, I'd like to know who she is."

"I don't mind at all. I want you to know everything there is to know about me. The woman in that picture was my best friend, Sarah. We grew up together."

CHAPTER 6

"I noticed you said was, did something happen?"

"She died about six years ago."

"I'm sorry to hear that. If anything ever happened to Porter I'd lose my mind. Was it an accident?"

"She was shot and killed on the streets."

"Wow, I'm really sorry. That's horrible."

"It was. I'd like to take you to my office today if you are up to it."

"I'd love to go and see what you do."

"We'll go shopping too. I noticed you packed light."

"It's kinda a shame leaving your home. It's so relaxing here."

"I say that just about every day. We don't have to go if you don't want to."

"No, I want to go."

"Good cause I cannot wait to show you something important."

"Do I get a hint?"

"Not this time, no."

She shakes her head with a smile on her face. Goddamn, she's so beautiful. It should be a crime for someone to be as beautiful as she is. I bet there are so many hearts she's broken that she doesn't even know it.

Ciara finished her tea while I went and took a shower. While she got ready to go, I called Becks to see if he'd be in the office. I would like him to be around to meet my girl. It's important to me that they get to know one another. Becks is a part of my daily life. I'm hoping Ciara becomes that too.

When I take Ciara out to the helicopter, she just gives me a look. I laugh. *"Don't you own a car or something?"*

"I do, but this is much faster and way more cool."

"Way more nerve wracking."

"The view will be worth it. I promise, nothing bad will happen to us."

She rolls her eyes then gets into the helicopter. Before she can panic more, I get us off the ground. Within minutes she is watching out the window as I tell her a few landmarks below. The flight to my building only takes us fifteen minutes. I land us safely on the rooftop.

"My heart is in my toes, but I gotta admit, it is kinda cool."

"Worth it, right?"

"Yes!"

We take a flight of stairs off the roof and enter my

building. I gave her a quick tour of the floor I occupy before showing her to my office. I tell her I own the entire building, but rent out office space to other businesses.

My office is a corner office. I like having as much of a view of the city as I can. I like being able to see the outside world as much as possible. I sit at my desk as Ciara checks out my space. I use this time to power on my computer. Just as it's turning on my phone begins to ring. Ciara being who she is tells me to go ahead and answer it. I already know it's Becks calling from the ring tone. We talk briefly and I look a few things up on the computer for him. Ciara is seated on the corner of my desk by the time Becks and I hang up the phone.

"Marshal business?"

"It was."

"I like your office. You sure do like a lot of windows. The view is great."

"Thanks. One cannot see the world if the view is blocked."

"So, what do you do here?"

"A little of this and a little of that."

"Oh, that is very telling."

"Well, you know how I bring fugitives in. Here I kinda do what I do for the Marshal, but it's not

always looking for a criminal. I search for lost family members or a friend. I also provide protection to victims by installing top of the line security equipment, bodyguards, or relocation. Whatever the client is looking for. I am very good at finding people. I will figure out who is after you, Ciara."

"Do you think Hunter is dangerous?"

"I don't really know for sure, yet. Tracking him has been a challenge. I could be way off, but I don't think he's the one."

"Who do you think it is then?"

"Here let me show you this." I bring up the tracking recording on my computer and show Ciara. I point out all the locations marked in red.

"What is all that?"

"I've been tracking a cell phone and all the red marks, they are places you have been."

"Whose number is it?"

"Your mothers."

"Oh."

"Has it stopped now that Grams gave her money?"

"She was in Vegas when you were there with Kirby."

"How does she keep knowing where I am going?"

"I am assuming the tabloids. A lot of my clients

are celebrities, they hire me because the media leads stalkers right to them. I prove they are a threat to my client and they get arrested."

"You said Hunter has been a challenge, how so?"

"Millie came to me after he showed up in Ohio when you were with Jasper. His cell phone hasn't left his apartment since he came back from Ohio. That is how I track a lot of people. I put a guy on him instead. I knew before he entered your store he was there."

"Where is my mother now?"

"Right now she is a few miles from Millie's."

"Are you watching anyone else?"

"Not really. Millie wanted me to track everyone that has had contact with you recently, including everyone you dated since January."

"She thought maybe one of the men that she auctioned me off to might have done this?"

"She wanted no stone left unturned. I even watched Porter."

"Wow!"

"You have nothing to worry about. It's none of them."

"That's a relief. Thank you for showing me this."

"You are welcome." I run a hand through my hair as I contemplate telling Ciara something that would

ease her mind. I want to think that I am the only guy in her life, but I know that isn't true. *"When we were in Vegas, you went to Kaiden's club. I saw how upset you were when the door was locked. I checked to see where his cell phone was located. He's in his hometown. He's been there a couple of weeks."*

"That's a huge relief, I was worried about him. I would feel really bad if something happened to him like it did Malcolm."

"I was hoping Becks would have been here to meet you. What do you say we go and do some shopping and then go back to my house?"

"I say let's do it."

I feel good about telling Ciara what I've been doing for her since last month. I hope she knows whoever is behind trying to destroy her livelihood, I will find out. I care about her deeply and that just makes me more determined.

CHAPTER SEVEN
CIARA

My mind has been put at ease knowing Wyatt is working hard to figure out who is behind vandalizing my store and apartment. It is troubling to know the prime suspect is my own mother. I cannot wrap my mind around why she would do this to me. I've been thinking about it for quite some time now. I've been wondering if maybe I should ask her myself. Have a little face to face chat with her. I want to see the expression on her face as I ask her why. Why go after me? I did nothing to her for her to come at me. I haven't laid eyes on her since I was around five. I want to know why she hates me as she does. If anyone should dislike someone it should be me hating her. I'm the one who was abandoned, not her. She's the one that made a choice. I had nothing to do with her decision.

Wyatt reaches across the kitchen counter that separates us and runs his fingers along my jaw. When they find my chin, he lifts my face so that I look at him. *"My beautiful girl is deep in thought. Tell me what's on your mind."*

"You told me your mother taught you how to make TV dinners, what did you mean by that?"

"It means she wasn't around much and when she was, she was tired."

"Why wasn't she around much?"

Wyatt comes around the counter to where I am. He takes my hand and we go to the living room. We sit next to each other on the sofa.

"When I was nine, I was sent to my room while some men in suits came to the house. I was supposed to close the door, but for some reason, I didn't. I was too curious about the men. I heard one of them ask my mother where my father was. She played dumb and asked them why they wanted to know. She denied knowing where he was when she knew. My father was a bad man. He had a violent side to him. I hated him. I was scared of him and so was my mother. The men that came to the house, one of them noticed me listening through the cracked door. On their way out, he stopped and asked if I knew where he was. I told

the guy the truth. He told me I was brave and was helping them get the bad guy."

"What did your mother do?"

"She didn't talk to me for a week. It wasn't until we were on our way to see my father that she spoke to me. She told me to keep my mouth shut. I wanted to be anywhere but in that car. I thought for sure they didn't catch him. I was scared to see him. Scared what he was going to do."

"So they didn't get him?"

"We arrived at the jail and I was happy my father was there. We sat across from him at a table. He looked me right in the eyes and blamed me for sending the marshals after him. I was glad he couldn't touch me or my mom. It meant my mom and I were safe. I knew in my gut he'd go too far one day and kill us as he did some guy."

"I'm sorry you had to go through all that."

"Because he was put away, he wasn't sending money home, so my mom worked two jobs. She was never around and when she was, she was too tired to be a mom."

Wyatt's striking blue eyes never lose their strength as he tells me that story. Wyatt is a man who has his shit together. Whatever he went through, he came out on top. I want that. I want to come out on top and have as much confidence as he does.

"Is that the reason you became a marshal?"

"It's the main reason. I saw a lot of crime growing up as well. Criminals need to be behind bars where they belong."

"Thank you for telling me all that."

"You are welcome. I better check on dinner."

Wyatt gets up from the sofa and goes to the kitchen. I let everything he told me sink in. The marshal was right, Wyatt was brave to snitch on his own father. That took a lot of courage for a young boy. I don't know if I could have done something like that if I were in the same situation.

"Wyatt," I say getting off the sofa and heading to the kitchen, *"what if I wanted to see my mother. Would you take me?"*

"If that is what you wish, yes. Nobody can stop you from seeing her except yourself or her. I would take you, but I don't believe at this time you should be alone with her because we are unsure if she's the one." He takes the food out of the oven and places it on the counter.

"I don't know yet if I want to see her."

"Take your time. It's a big decision. I do want to

say, it could give you some closure you may have needed all these years."

I think Wyatt is right, I shouldn't go alone. I don't think I would want to go with anyone other than him. He's already proven to me that he has my best interest at heart. If I end up with him, I know that he'll have my back no matter what life throws at me.

We take our dinner plates to the roof and eat while watching the sunset. These men that Grams set me up with all have gorgeous homes. Wyatt's place is no different. I love it here and feel right at home. If I do end up with him, I could see myself living here. I wouldn't even ask him to think about moving to New York. This place is him through and through.

After our dinner is done, we move to a lounge chair. Instead of lounging on my own, I curl up with him and we watch the stars. He tells me about the neighbor lady and how she became part of his life. Wyatt was about twelve when he was starting to hang out with the wrong crowd. He was dragged home one night by a cop after a fight broke out on the street. Of course, his mother wasn't home, so she stepped in. From that day on, she taught him many life lessons. One being you can be a criminal or you can fight and not become one. She was the one that helped him see the future. Because of that lady, he turned out to be a good man, he said. He spent so much time at her house, that is how he and Sarah become best friends. With or without the neighbor lady, I believe Wyatt still would have turned out to be the man he is. He's had it in him ever since he turned his own father into the marshals.

CHAPTER EIGHT
WYATT

My time with Ciara is flying by faster than I want. I cannot believe we are fast approaching two weeks together. Being with her is easy. We have many deep conversations. I love hearing about her days in high school being on the swim team and how she realized she would follow in Millie's footsteps by becoming a clothing designer. Everything about her is easy to love. The hardest part about all of this is knowing she might not pick me in the end. It will devastate me if she doesn't. I have fallen for this woman hard. I want to be with her for life. Ciara compliments my life very well. I would go as far as saying she's the last missing piece of me. She completes me in a way that I didn't really realize was missing. I haven't ever felt this way in my entire life.

In the time we've been together, we have only left

my home the one time I took her to my office. We don't need fancy dinners out or extravagant dates to enjoy each other's company. The fact that we can stay in to cook, watch movies, or enjoy an evening on the roof together says a lot about how well we get along. I would rather have a million more conversations with Ciara than have anything else this world has to offer.

Ciara and I did some hiking today around my property. While she went to take a shower, I set up dinner for us on the roof. We already missed the sunset because we were gone so long today. By the time we got back and got dinner going it was getting dark. We might have made it back in time if we could keep our hands off one another. Sex on our hike was worth missing one sunset for. Besides having conversation, Ciara and I have a strong sexual chemistry. I couldn't even begin to tell you how many times we've had sex. Every time we think we've had enough of each other, we go at it again. Sex on the roof, on the sofa, the kitchen counter, the hiking trail, and the bedroom, it doesn't matter to us where our clothes come off.

"Oh, Wyatt, it's beautiful."

I turn toward her coming onto the roof. This table I set is nothing compared to the beautiful sight of her.

She gives me a kiss before picking up the flowers I put on the table and smells them.

"Dinner should be ready in a few minutes."

"I can't believe you picked all these today and made such a gorgeous bouquet out of them."

"I really didn't do anything to them besides put them in the vase."

"You did a remarkable job, so take the compliment."

I pull out the chair for Ciara to sit at the table, then open a bottle of wine and pour our glasses. *"Relax while I go and get our dinner."*

She nods her head and I sneak in a kiss before I leave the rooftop. Ciara doesn't have to tell me something is weighing heavy on her mind today. I can already tell by her demeanor when we were on our hike and still at this moment. I'm going to wait until she's ready to talk about it. I'm hoping she doesn't keep holding it in much longer. I can't help her with whatever it is if she doesn't tell me.

I plate our food and take it to our table. The food looks delicious. I have enjoyed teaching Ciara how to cook my favorite dishes. She seems to enjoy it just as much as I do.

"Your dinner, my lady."

"You keep teaching me all these yummy foods to eat, I'm going to gain a shit ton of weight."

"Nah, sex is the one of the best exercise, so we'll just keep doing that."

"Now that, you won't hear any complaints from me." I laugh. *"So there's something I want to ask you."* I get an alert on my phone that someone is at my door. Becks has horrible timing. *"Is that your friend?"*

"Yes."

"Invite him up. I want to meet him."

"You were about to ask me something."

"It can wait until later."

I use the app on my phone and tell Becks we are on the roof. *"I'm sorry he is stopping by during our dinner."*

"Really, it's not a problem. I've been wanting to meet him. It will be nice putting a face to your friend that you talk so much about."

"Oh dear, I'm interrupting your dinner."

"Becks, this is the lovely Ciara Verbank. Ciara, Andrew Becks."

"It's lovely to finally meet you," Becks says to my girl.

"I can say the same. Wyatt has told me so much

about you. You should join us for dinner," Ciara tells him.

"I'll go and make you a plate."

"I really don't want to intrude."

"You are not intruding. I've been looking forward to someone telling me about the guy I'm dating." Ciara giggles.

"Then it's settled. Becks pull up a seat and I'll be right back with your plate."

"Here, take this with you. It's everything you asked for."

He hands me a folder. Ciara's brows raise. I know she is curious about what's inside it. I am eager myself to see what he found out for me. I called in a favor with Becks to do some digging for me. My fingers are crossed he got what I was looking for. I would have done it myself, but that would have required me to leave Ciara for a day and I wasn't about to do that.

I open the folder and skim through it real quick. It looks as though Becks came through for me. I am very pleased. I'm also wondering how he got this information. It's more than I thought he'd get. I owe him for this even though I said I was calling in a favor. I put the folder inside my briefcase that's in my home office. Ciara doesn't go in there much. I don't need her seeing this before I do some digging myself. I am not about to take this information and run with it until I have all the facts straight.

※

Ciara seemed to really enjoy Becks company. That's a huge relief because if we end up together, they'll be seeing each other often. It's always nice when your buddy and girl get along. The last girl I dated didn't like Becks at all. I believe the feelings were mutual. It doesn't matter because obviously that relationship didn't work out.

At one point Ciara went to get us another bottle of wine. I took that time with Becks to ask him how he got the information I saw in the folder. He told me he took a page out of my book and went for it. I laughed and then asked which page he was referring to. All he told me it was the one where you get cozy with the person you want info from. Then he flat laughed and said, 'boy was she pissed when I paid my tab and left without her.'

It is late and Becks finally just left. I'm happy to have my girl curled up next to me. I could literally do this the rest of my life. At the end of the month, my bed is not going to feel the same.

"Comfortable?"

"Very much so."

"You were going to ask me something earlier, what was it?"

Ciara lifts off my chest and rests on her elbow. *"I thought long and hard about this. Can you take me to see my mother?"*

"I can. I need you to mentally prepare yourself that it might not go the way you want."

"I know. I've come to the conclusion I won't know what will happen if I don't try."

I lean forward and kiss her forehead. *"I'll get it set up."*

"Thank you."

She settles her body into mine. I have my work cut out for me tomorrow. Tomorrow would be a great day for her to sleep in.

CHAPTER NINE
CIARA

It never fails that I wake to an empty bed. These men that Grams auction me off to are always up before me. It would be nice to wake in the arms of at least one of them. Wyatt I swear doesn't sleep at all. He's always slipping out of bed after I fall asleep. He doesn't think I know it, but I do. It doesn't wake me fully, but I feel the loss of him when he is gone. I curl right back up to his body as soon as he comes back to bed. I sleep better when he's next to me, even if it's only for a couple of hours.

I do my normal thing when I get out of bed, go out to the kitchen and turn the burner on for hot water. Wyatt always has the tea kettle ready for me so that I only need to heat the water. I pick through the flavors as I wait. This morning he put out donuts, so I opened the box and pick a powdered, jelly filled one. As I bite into it, the fruity flavor of raspberry fills my tastebuds. It's like having a piece of heaven in my mouth. It isn't by any means Katie's fresh muffins but it's a wonderful substitute. I make my tea while I eat the donut. I figured Wyatt would be on the roof as he is every morning, but there is a light drizzle out. I take my tea with me in one hand and my half eaten breakfast in the other as I search for him. I figure he's in his home office since he's not out in the open floor plan. When I get to the doorway, he looks to be concentrating on whatever is on his computer. He doesn't even seem to notice me. I lean on the doorframe and watch him for a minute. I have a feeling he's not the type to do his job half-assed. I bet he has all his T's crossed and I's dotted before going after a criminal or whatever he's working on.

Wyatt is such a handsome man. He takes his glasses off and leans his head back, rubbing his face with his hands. His bare upper body is bulging with muscles. Besides looking handsome and hot as hell, he looks overworked. I would know, I used to carry the same look before Grams sold me to ten highest bidders.

I tiptoe into the room, setting my tea on the desk. He hurry's and closes the web browser. I put a hand on his shoulders.

"I think you need a break from working."

My hand falls from his shoulder as he swivels his chair around. Wyatt, puts his hands on my waist and pulls me onto his lap. My hand accidentally goes between his legs and he winks at me. He takes the uneaten part of my donut from my hand, putting it to my lips. I take a bite then he kisses me. The flavor of him mixed with raspberry is divine. I squeal when he lifts me off his lap and begins to carry me out of the office.

"Where are you taking me?"

"Back to bed."

"I'm not tired."

"Who said anything about sleeping?"

"Mr. Bradshaw, are you trying to get morning nookie?"

We are both laughing about my comment as Wyatt keeps walking toward his room. He puts me to my feet once we are near his bed. He cups both sides of my face with his hands and his striking blue eyes connect with mine. His expression turns serious.

"Is everything alright?"

"Do you have any idea how much you mean to me?"

"I think so."

"I'm in love with you, Ciara." I open my mouth to say something, but his finger goes to my lips before

a word can form. *"I don't want morning nookie, I want to make love to you and show you how much you mean to me."*

His finger is still on my lips, so I just nod my head. When his lips meet mine, I get lost in it. This kiss is soft and loving. Nothing like how he's kissed me before. I feel the love pouring out of him as his body moves in closer. I start to wonder what has brought this on. Then I tell myself to leave it alone and get lost in this man that I'm falling for. Wyatt Bradshaw makes that part easy. I can tell he has a lot of love to give. There isn't a single thing about him I'd change. That is what makes this relationship so real. Nobody should have to change who they are to be with someone they love.

My head leans back as Wyatt's mouth is on the front of my neck. His lips are tender upon my skin, sending goosebumps all over my flesh. When he unties my robe, he watches my eyes. I get chills as the front of my robe falls open. His eyes travel from mine to my breasts back to my eyes. His hand slides from my side to my back, tugging me in closer to him. His free hand holds my jawline as he kisses me again. I feel the tingling between my legs. I want Wyatt inside of me, showing me how much he loves me. I already know his manhood is hard because I can feel it pressed between our bodies. Without a second thought I slip my hands into his waistband and push his pajamas pants past his hips. His hands slide the robe off my shoulders. The loss of his mouth on mine allows me to take a deep breath. I moan when his lips kiss my shoulders. My robe falls to the floor just before he lifts me off my feet and cradles me in his arms. Wyatt lays my naked body on the bed. I bite my bottom lip as he finishes removing his pants. I spread my legs, thinking he's going to get between them, but he doesn't. Instead he lies next to me. I watch as his hand goes to my stomach.

"I could spend the rest of my life just looking at you and I'd be happy. You're beautiful, Ciara, inside and out. I consider myself lucky to have this opportunity to be with you. I thought my life was complete then you came waltzing in and showed me it wasn't complete without you. I will spend the rest of my days on this earth showing you how much I am in love with you if you choose me."

"I ...,"

"Shh," he says.

His fingertips lightly trace up my body, leaving a trail of goosebumps behind. *"I can already feel you love me, so you don't have to tell me in words. Show me by coming back here to live and becoming my wife."*

"Wyatt..."

My words are hushed by his mouth on mine. His palm glides down my body, then his fingers massage my clit. My body reacts to his words, to his touch. I have fallen in love with Wyatt. I think I understand why he doesn't want to hear I love him, too. He thinks actions speak louder than words. In this situation, he is right. I have told some of the other men I love them without proving to them that I do. I can only show one of these men how true my love is for them and that it's real love. I feel selfish for expressing my love for them. Tears fill my eyes. I hate that I'm going to cause heartache to the ones that found love with me and I don't return the same love they deserve. I don't like hurting people. I know how that feels to get your hopes up that you finally found the right person and then they drop you like a hot coal is burning your skin.

Wyatt wipes my tears away with his thumb. I sit up, bending my knees up, and rest my forehead on them. *"I'm a horrible person."*

"That is untrue. You are the most real person I know."

"I'm going to hurt people. That makes me a horrible person."

"Ciara, all ten of us guys knew what we were getting into when we put our bid in to date you. I can't speak for any of them, but I can for myself. If I get my heart broken, it was a risk worth taking. I wouldn't trade a moment of our time together for anything. I have absolutely no regrets."

"If I don't come back here to be with you, can you say the same thing to me? I don't think you will be able to. If you love me as you say, you will probably wish you saved your money and your heart from being broken."

"You should know by now I'm not the type of person to blow smoke up someone's ass. I do as I say and say what I mean. I will have no regrets about being with you. Have I fallen in love with you? Yes. Will I be hurt if we don't end up together? Yes. All that doesn't change my decision on dating you."

Wyatt gets off the bed and puts his pajamas pants on. He bends to get my robe, then hands it to me. My overactive mind ruined what was going to be a beautiful, unforgettable moment between us.

"I'm sorry, Wyatt. I didn't mean to ruin something I know would have been wonderful between us."

CHAPTER 9

"Come with me," he says, holding his hand out for me to take, *"I want to show you something."*

I put my hand in his as I get off the bed, then put my robe on and tie the strap. He takes my hand, lacing our fingers together as we leave his bedroom. The very bedroom I could possibly be sharing with him in the future.

We go to his office and he sits behind his desk. *"I know you saw the folder Becks gave me. I want to show you what was in it, but first I need to tell you what I asked him to do for me."*

My heart skips a few beats and my stomach knots. His tone of voice is serious. I'm not sure I can handle whatever he's about to show me. What if it's something bad? My mind is already a jumbled mess and I don't think I can handle any more confusion. But it could be something good, right? I just wish I could rewind the time and go back to what we were doing before I started overthinking. I straighten my back. I need to just shut my mind off and hear what he needs to tell me.

"What is it you need to tell me?"

"I asked Becks to do something I would do myself if I wanted inside information."

I try to think about the kind of questions Becks asked me when he was here. Nothing really pops out at me. *"Okay, just tell me already. I feel like I did something wrong again."*

"You have done nothing wrong. I might have been the one who has, though."

"I highly doubt that."

"I asked Becks to get cozy with your mother to find out if she'd spill her guts to him."

"What do you mean by cozy?"

"He followed her to a bar, bought her drinks and showed her he was interested in sleeping with her."

"He slept with her?"

"No, only bought her enough drinks to get her talking."

"Did he find out if she's the one who destroyed my store?"

"He asked her if she had children and when she said yes, he kept pressing her for more information. Ciara, he got out of her the name of who she believes is your father."

I grab onto the desk as my knees go weak. I think I'm going to be sick. What gives him the right to invade in my past like this? What if I don't want to know who fathered me?

My voice cracks when I say, *"What gives you the right to do that? What if I don't ever want to know?"*

"I did it because I love you. I can see firsthand

that you struggle with how you think you'll be a bad parent or even a wife because you think you are like your mother. You need the truth to move past being abandoned by her and not knowing all these years if your father abandoned you as well. If you don't want what I found, I'll keep it to myself." I take a deep breath, not knowing if I want to know any more. *"Before you give me your answer, you need to know she told Becks that she never told the man she was pregnant with you. He doesn't know about you."*

"My mother is a lair. She could have told Becks a fictional story because she gets off on telling lies."

"I don't believe she lied to him."

"Why would you say that? You don't know her. Hell, I don't even know her. I only go off by what Grams says."

"You are right, I don't know her."

I walk away from his desk. Why has he opened this can of worms? I pace the floor as I let everything sink in. He gives me the space I need.

After I spend the next few minutes trying to control my thoughts, I spin on my heels and stare at him. I do know one thing and that's that I know Wyatt. He'd never intentionally hurt. He probably knows me better than I know myself. What if he's right and I do need this closure to better myself?

"Why do you believe she didn't lie to Becks?"

"Because I searched him and you are a spitting image of him. I think your mother has known all this time who your father is."

I never thought I looked anything like my mother. *"If who you found is my father and he knows nothing about me, how does that help me?"*

"If you choose to confront him, you'll know for sure if he knew about you or not."

"If he has known about me all these years and abandoned me like she did, how does that help me better myself?"

"Because you'll see who you don't want to be and be a better person for it. Just like it did for me to see my father in jail." Wyatt gets up from behind the desk and comes to where I am across the room. He reaches up and holds my jawline. *"There is always the possibility of you two becoming father and daughter."*

"I can't take the chance of being rejected."

"He'd be a fool to reject you. I'm going to leave you alone and give you some time to think about what you want to do. The pin to my computer is written on a piece of paper on the desk if you want to look at what I found out. I'll be around the house when you are ready to come out."

Wyatt gives me a kiss on my forehead before he

leaves me with my thoughts in his office. I collapse in a chair the moment he is gone. I seriously think I'm going to be sick. How in the world am I going to decide on what to do? I have all kinds of emotions inside me, spinning around in circles, getting knotted and entangled with one another. I have no idea which emotion to act on.

CHAPTER TEN
CIARA

I have been sitting in the same place for hours. The rain hasn't let up at all. Even though I know I should go back inside, my body seems to not want to move. I'm not avoiding Wyatt. He isn't the reason I haven't gotten out of the rain. I finally feel like my mind has shut off and I want it to stay that way. I don't want to think about anything. Not my mother, who my father is. Hell, I don't even want to think about my store. I just wanted to sit out here and stare off into the beautiful world that is surrounding me with all its peaceful grace. I wish I could snap my fingers and feel this calm all the time. Maybe it's not calmness, it's numbness instead.

When I left Wyatt's office and came to the roof. I didn't care if it was still drizzling out or not. I felt like I was suffocating in that office. Knowing that I could finally find out who my father is after all these years of not knowing scared the ever living shit out of me. I felt like I couldn't breathe. When I was little I often wondered what my father looked like, what his laugh was like, what it would feel like to hug him. I wanted to know if he'd protect me from the big, bad world and love me as a father should? To find out he might not have known about me at all, is a whole new troubling thought. I have no idea how he would react to finding out I'm his daughter. Would he deny it or open his arms and welcome me into his life? I don't think I am strong enough to find out. I can't take any more rejection in my heart. My mother did enough damage all on her own. Just knowing one of your parents didn't want you is enough pain to last any kid a lifetime. If I knew for sure he didn't want me, it would crush me. I think not knowing if he did or didn't is easier to live with.

What Wyatt did for me was the kindest thing anyone has ever done for me. I love him that much more for caring about me this much. I understand what he is saying to me about needing closure. A big part of me agrees with him. However, I don't think it's my father I need that with. It's my mother. She's the one that carried me for nine months. She's also the one that chose to walk away before I was five. I want to know why. If she could ever tell me any kind of truth, that's what I want to know.

"Ciara, you should really get out of the rain."

I have no idea how long Wyatt has been on the roof. I didn't hear him come up. He could have been standing behind me for hours and I don't think I would have known. I only realized he was here by the sound of his voice.

"I don't think I could move even if I wanted to."

He comes to my side and takes one look at me. My clothes are soaked through. I'm sure my eyes are puffy and red from crying.

"I'm sorry, Ciara. If I had known this would put you in this state, I would have kept my nose out of your business. I feel horrible."

I take his hand. *"I'm not upset with you. If anything I'm grateful to know you care enough about me to help me get over my past. It's all just a hard pill to swallow."*

"Let me get you out of this rain. I drew you a hot bath."

I nod my head and before I can get out of this chair I'm glued to, he bends down and swoops me into his arms. I put my arm around him and bury my face in the crook of his neck. His scent in my nose is calming. I cannot deny I have fallen for him. I also cannot deny how safe I feel when I'm with him. I know Wyatt would protect me even if it meant getting himself hurt in the process. Without a doubt in my mind, I know he'd give his life for mine. I don't think I've met anyone before that I felt that kind of safety with. Well, anyone besides Grams. She's always been my protector.

Wyatt sets me to my feet, then unties my soaked robe and removes it from my body. I step into the hot bath and he turns the jets on. I don't want him to leave me, so I reach up and grab his hand.

"I don't want to be alone."

"Okay, I'll sit right here with you."

He sits on the side of the tub. I get up to my knees and take the hem of his shirt in my hands. *"Get in with me?"*

He stands and removes his clothes. I move so that he has room to sit in the water. Once he is settled into the water, he takes hold of one of my feet and starts massaging the bottom. I lean my head back and close my eyes. I felt some of the stress melting away. If I feel anything at all for the rest of the night, I want it to be him. Everything else going on in my life can be kept in silent mode.

I keep my eyes closed and my head back while Wyatt massaged both of my feet. The water has begun to turn cold. I sit up and get to my knees. Wyatt's eyes stay on mine. I take his hand and put it between my legs. My head falls back as his fingers enter me and his thumb plays with my clit. I need this release. I need all the built up tension to leave my body.

I lift my head and look right at him. *"Take me to bed, Wyatt. I want you to fuck me hard until we both cum."* When he is searching my face for the right answer because I don't talk like that, I say, *"Please."*

"Stand up, Ciara."

I do as he says and he lifts my foot, setting it on the tub's edge. When he leans forward and takes my clit between his lips, I moan. I put a hand on the wall to stabilize my body's weight as his face moves to be in between my legs. His tongue dips inside me and it feels incredible. My mind is completely turned off. I don't want anything to disrupt this feeling.

Between my wet skin and what Wyatt is doing to my body, my flesh is coated with goosebumps. I am so damn turned on by it all. My knees became unstable the closer I come to a release. When his mouth is gone from my pussy, I groan. He puts my foot down before he gets to his feet. I squeal when he puts me over his shoulder and carries me to his bed. My body bounces on the mattress. I'm on my back for only a split second before he rolls me over and yanks my hips up so that my ass is in the air. I brace myself for the impact of his cock entering me in a forceful way. I asked for it, it's what I want. I need it.

My body jolts forward as he penetrates me from behind. No amount of the tight grip on the blankets would stop my body from moving forward. I moan letting him know it's what I want. Wyatt doesn't hold back, he thrusts into me hard over and over. It's exactly what I asked for. I am nowhere ready to give him my orgasm. I moan as his cock goes deep inside me and he holds himself there. My upper body is lifted off the mattress and Wyatt kisses my shoulder, my neck and then I feel his breath next to my ear.

"Is this what you want, Ciara?"

"Yes."

Wyatt turns my head so that he can kiss me. I moan into his mouth as his hands cup my breasts and his fingers pinch my nipples. When his mouth leaves mine, he pushes my body back to the bed, flipping me over. I stare up at him. His blue eyes travel all over my naked body. It sends shivers down my spine. He bends over top of me and hovers his weight above me. I close my eyes as he gently enters me. I feel his breath upon my neck as his body presses into mine. Wyatt is no longer fucking me, he's making love to me. With each gentle thrust, I become that much closer to release. I thought I knew what I wanted, but I didn't. Wyatt making love to me is what I needed.

※

After Wyatt and I had sex we cuddled for the longest time. We talked a little about nothing really. It was more like small talk. I heard his breathing change as he drifted off to sleep. I stayed snuggled up next to him unable to find sleep myself. It didn't take long for my mind to start wandering. At first I thought about how well Wyatt and I get along. I started picturing myself moving here and him putting a ring on my finger. We haven't talked about having children, but I could see him being a wonderful father. I still have doubts about myself as a parent. I thought back to when I was with Malcolm and how I didn't have these kinds of doubts. It seems the more I fall in love with these men, the more unsure I have become about myself as a mother. I realized Wyatt is completely right, I do need closure to my past to be able to be a better person.

I slipped out of bed and tiptoed out of the bedroom. I came to Wyatt's office and turned on the desk light. I've been staring at the computer and the pin written on a piece of paper, trying to get the courage to see who my father is.

My hands are shaking as I hit the power button. When the screen lights up, I punch in the first three numbers. I tell myself I can do this and that I need this so that I can build a better future. When I hit the last number, the computer automatically turns on. Wyatt was looking at my father when I came into his office this morning. My stomach turns as I stare at the picture. I do look just like him as Wyatt said. I take hold of the mouse to begin reading. My father's name appears just below his picture. *"Ciaro Kirkwood,"* I say his name out loud a few times. My mother must have really cared about him to practically give me his name. He appears to be a bit older than her. I wonder if that had anything to do with her not telling him about me.

I close out the browser without reading about the man who impregnated my mother. I don't care to learn about him off the internet. There's only one way for me to know what happened the night I was created. I get up from the desk and turn the light off, then head back to bed to be with Wyatt. I need to sleep on what I'm going to do next.

CHAPTER ELEVEN
CIARA

My month with Wyatt has gone by way too fast. I cannot believe I will be going home today. Our time together isn't ending, he'll be coming with me to Grams later tonight. Yesterday I finally told him I saw who my father is on his computer. I am not ready to go to Ciaro and tell him I'm his long lost daughter. I am ready to confront my mother, though. I have thought long and hard about seeing her. I know there is no way of knowing how it will work out between us until we are face to face. I'm not holding my hand on my ass for a good outcome. The things I've heard about her, she isn't all that great of a person. Especially if she's the one that wrecked my store and burnt Malcolm's home. God only knows what else she's done in the last twenty years since she left.

I find Wyatt on the rooftop. He was showered and

CHAPTER 11

ready to go before I even had my tea. I walk up behind him and put my arms around his waist, resting my cheek on his back. I breathe in the fresh air mixed with him. I can honestly say I'm going to miss being at Wyatt's home. Of all the places I've been, this has by far been my favorite place.

"Are you ready?"

"I think so."

Wyatt turns around to face me. *"I'm going to miss seeing you coming up here every morning."*

I smile. *"I'm going to miss it, too."*

"I think today is going to make a new beginning for your future."

I wrap my arms around him again. This time his heart beats beneath my ear. He rests his chin on the top of my head. I'm not ready to let him go just yet. I could stand here all day like this.

"Wyatt, thank you for everything you do for me."

"You are welcome." He lifts my face so that I must look at him. *"I'd do anything for you. You know that, right?"*

"I do."

"I bought this place two years after I started my business. I love it here. It's the first place I ever felt like I was home. I'd give it up for you if it meant we'd be together."

"I would never ask you or want you to do that for me." I get up on my tiptoes and kiss him. *"It's home."*

"I hope that's true."

I leave his arms and move to see the view before we leave. Wyatt's arms wrap around my upper body. I love it when he holds me. I feel loved and protected when he does.

I point out toward the helicopter. *"I assume that's our ride?"*

"You assumed right."

"Lovely."

He laughs at my sarcasm and so do I. I laugh because it still makes me nervous. I trust Wyatt with my life, but it doesn't make me love flying. At this point, nothing probably will.

❧

Wyatt and I landed safely on the ground about twenty minutes ago. We are now in my car heading to where my mother is. Her cell phone is telling us she is at McCally's bar and grill. The closer we get, the more my hands sweat and I feel shaky inside. I keep reminding myself to just breathe. I am strong enough to face my mother.

"Remember, I'll be at the bar and if you need me, just get up and walk toward me. My eyes are never going to leave you."

"Okay," I say with my voice cracking.

"It's not too late, you can change your mind if you want."

"No, it's time to get this done and over with. This probably should have been done a long time ago."

I get out of the car before I change my mind. Once I am inside I see my mother sitting at a table with a gentleman. I walk over to where she is with my head held high.

"Cassidy."

Her head turns to look over her shoulder. *"Well I'll be damned, my daughter has come to find me."*

I look at the gentleman sitting with her. *"Can I have a moment alone with Cassidy please."*

"Look at you being all formal and calling me by my given name. Most people who know me call me Cassy."

"I don't know you."

"Right! So I would assume you don't want a hug from your mother?"

"Ya, I'll pass."

"A happy family reunion is out of the question, so what brings you here?"

"Why did you leave me?"

She laughs with her husky, smokers laugh. *"Are you complaining that I left you in good hands? As far as I can see you turned out pretty damn well. Millie got what she wanted in you that she couldn't have out of me."*

"What's that supposed to mean?"

"Your dear, beloved grandmother couldn't turn me into her, but she sure did turn my offspring into herself. Millie Verbank clothing line ended up staying in the family after all."

My voice raises when I say, *"Are you always this much of a bitch?"*

"Not always. I tend to get bitchy when someone is bothering me when I don't want to be bothered."

"If you'd just answer my questions, I won't bother you again."

"I left you because I didn't want you. I thought I did at first, but goddamn you looked too much like the sperm donor."

"Did you love him?"

"Didn't Millie tell you? I don't love anyone but myself."

"You can sit here and play victim all you want, but being an asshole to me isn't going to happen." I lean forward over the table between us. *"I know it*

was you who vandalized my store. I'm going to prove it and send you to jail."

"Is that a secret?" She narrows her eyes at me and I see her shoulders drop. *"Yes, I loved the man who fathered you. I never got the chance to tell him about you because he left the states."*

"Where did he go?"

"Paris, his friends told me. He left to study clothing design. I never bothered to find him."

"Why did you come after me?"

"I needed the money. What Millie gives me monthly isn't enough. I knew my dear mother would give it to me if I'd stop bothering you."

I had no idea Grams gives my mother money every month. It's quite shocking really. *"Why do you need so much money?"*

"Life has a way of dealing its own karma."

"Are you in trouble?"

"If you call dying trouble, then yes, I'm in trouble."

"Do you have cancer?"

"No. I am in kidney failure. I need the money for treatment until my name is put on the donor list."

"I'm sorry to hear that."

"I don't deserve your sympathy, Ciara. Don't be running your mouth to Millie about why I needed the

money. You two would be better off without ever seeing me again."

I sit here stunned by what she is saying. All the while in the back of my mind, I know she's a liar. I have no idea if she's telling me the truth or not.

"Next time you need money, ask for it instead of ruining my store. Don't be burning down anymore homes while you're at."

"I didn't burn down anyone's home. I did do your store and followed you around, but I didn't light any fires."

"I should go."

"Ciaro Kirkwood is your father's name. You sure do look just like him." I get to my feet. *"I'm sorry, Ciara, for the pain I may have caused you. I didn't know what else to do. I started following you because I admired your life. Millie never would have done for me what she did for you. She hated every boy I ever brought home and I couldn't ever live up to her standards."*

"Cassidy, Grams only wanted you to apply yourself to something you loved. You didn't have to follow in her footsteps to be someone great. You have to at some point in life take responsibility for your own actions. Stop blaming Grams for how your life turned out because that's all on you. I hope you get well."

She grabs my hand. *"Wait,"* when I look at her hand on mine she releases it, *"I want to see you again. Can we go out to lunch or dinner sometime? You're my daughter."*

"Right now we aren't even friends let alone mother and daughter."

"Please."

"I'll think about it."

Wyatt gets up from the bar and meets me halfway. We leave and I couldn't be more proud of the way I handled myself. I fucking did it! I don't care if I ever see her again. My mother is a narcissistic bitch. I am happy to know she didn't raise me.

I threw myself in Wyatt's arms and kissed him. *"I love you, Wyatt Bradshaw."*

"I love you, Ciara Verbank."

We go back to Grams to have dinner with her. Honestly, I cannot wait to be alone with Wyatt. I have three more days before I go off and meet the last guy I must date for a month. I have every intention of using my time with Wyatt wisely. I am hoping that Jeremy is coming with me to Adler Vaughn's home.

ABOUT THE AUTHOR

Thank you so much for taking the time to read Grandma's Silent Auction - September. Word-of-mouth is crucial for any author to succeed. If you enjoyed the book, please leave a review on Amazon. Even if it's just a sentence or two. It would make all the difference and would be very much appreciated. – OXOX Michael James

Michael's Links:

Website: http://michaeljames-author332.bravesites.com/

ALSO BY MICHAEL JAMES

If you enjoyed Grandma's Silent Auction - September, you may also like my other books:

The Way We Love series:

Pink Skies At Night

Shadows At Night

Nights Are Unlimited

Concealed By The Night

Shattered At Night

Freed At Night

Winning A Cowgirl's Heart - Trilogy:

The Rodeo King

The Best Friend

The Fate Of My Heart

Winning a Cowgirl's Heart -Complete Box Set

Construction Vs. Corporate- Trilogy:

Unbalanced

Balancing

Balanced

Secrets Within a Club

Club Comrade

Revenge

Saving Club Conrad

Masquerade Saga

His Pearls

His Secrets

His Prison

His Games

His Moves

All His

Crime in Landkaster series

The Mirror

Times Like These

Lonely Road of Faith

Grandma's Silent Auction series

January

February

March

April

May

June

July

August

Lost Love Letter

I'll be Waiting

Before I Do

Standalone:

Toying With October

Pieces Of Me

A Christmas For Eve

Dom Diaries: Tangled Up In You

Christmas Scavenger Hunt

Blue Christmas

Stealing the Christmas Spotlight

Co-written with Jodi Fahey

Last Sheet

Co-written with Daniel Grayson

Inside the Storm

Manufactured by Amazon.ca
Bolton, ON

44882441R00059